# Bubba and Beau
## Best Friends

Kathi Appelt        Arthur Howard



Voyager Books
Harcourt, Inc.
*Orlando   Austin   New York   San Diego   Toronto   London*

*To Gary and Sandi and all their hound-puppies —K. A.*

*To Allyn, who hounded me to do it —A. H.*



www.HarcourtBooks.com 

First Voyager Books edition 2006

*Voyager Books* is a trademark of Harcourt, Inc., registered in the United States of America and/or other jurisdictions.

The Library of Congress has cataloged the hardcover edition as follows:
Appelt, Kathi, 1954–
Bubba and Beau, best friends/Kathi Appelt; illustrated by Arthur Howard.
p. cm.
Summary: When Mama Pearl washes their favorite blanket it's a sad day for best friends Bubba and Beau, but it gets worse when she decides the baby boy and his puppy need baths, too.
[1. Best friends–Fiction. 2. Cleanliness–Fiction. 3. Babies–Fiction. 4. Dogs–Fiction.]
I. Howard, Arthur, ill. II. Title.
PZ7.A6455Bu 2002
[E]–dc21 2001001987
ISBN-13: 978-0152-02060-6 ISBN-10: 0-15-202060-8
ISBN-13: 978-0152-05580-6 pb ISBN-10 0-15-205580-0 pb

H G F E D C B A

The display type was set in Cloister Oldstyle Bold.
The text type was set in Cloister Oldstyle.
Color separations by Bright Arts Ltd., Hong Kong
Manufactured by South China Printing Company, Ltd., China
Production supervision by Ginger Boyer
Designed by Arthur Howard and Judythe Sieck

# Chapter One

Meet Bubba.

Bubba is the son of Big Bubba and Mama Pearl.

Right after Bubba was born, Mama Pearl wrapped him in his soft pink blankie and whispered into both of his soft pink ears, "I love you, Bubba Junior." She sighed. He was the perfect little Bubba.

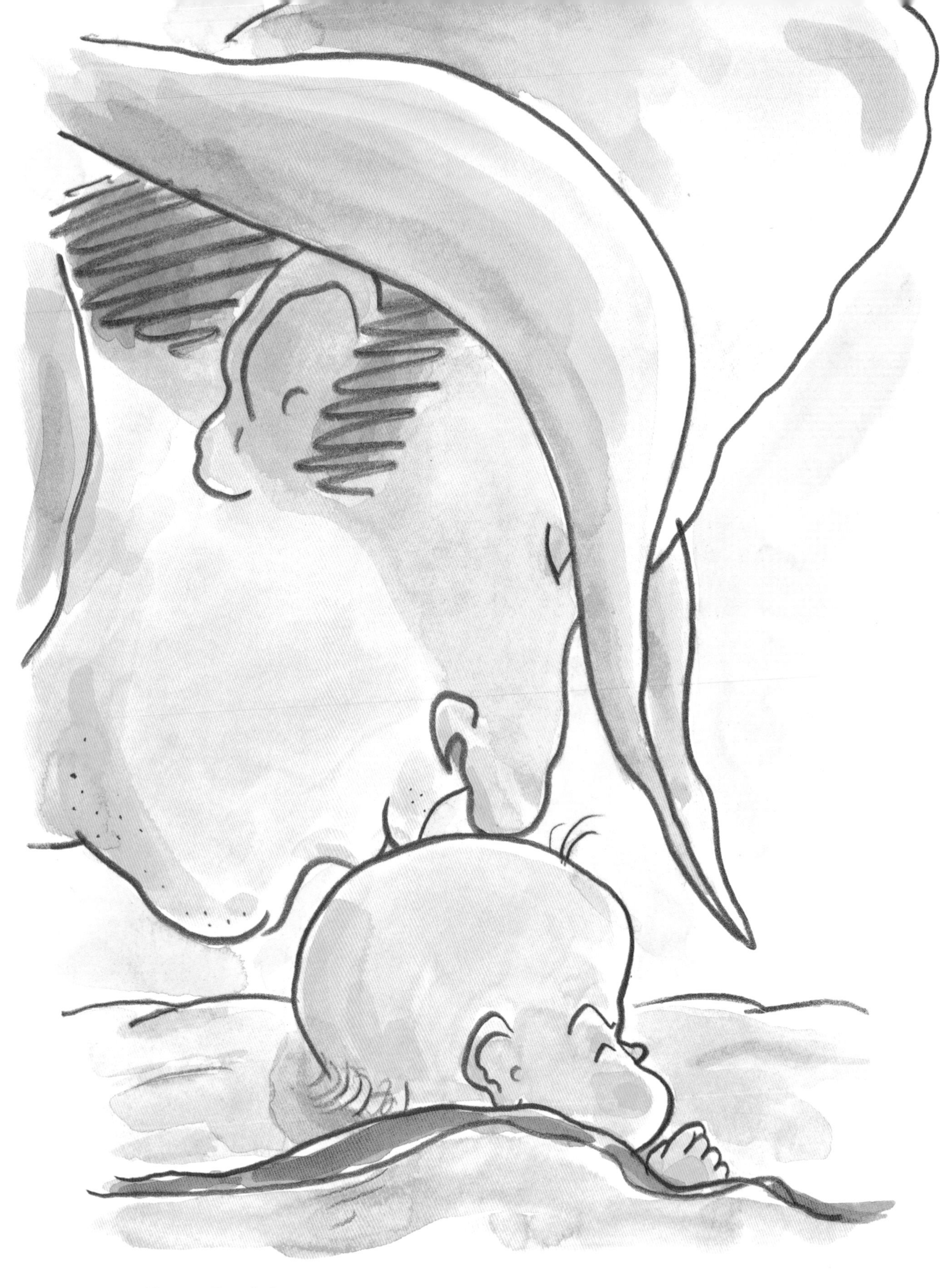

Big Bubba was just plumb tickled! He kissed that boy right on the top of his head.

Then, because he was so excited, he went outside and revved up Earl, his trusty pickup truck, and honked the horn as loud as he could.

*Toot! Toot! Tooooooooot!*

# Chapter Two

Meet Beau.

Beau is the puppy of Maurice and Evelyn.

When Beau was born, Evelyn licked him from the top of his teeny round ears to the tip of his tiny red tail. She sighed. He was the perfect little hound-puppy.

Maurice was downright delighted. He ran around and around the yard in circles. Finally, he couldn't stand it any longer. He threw back his head and began to bay.

*Ar-ar-arooooooo!!!*

One perfect baby. One perfect hound.
And a lot of commotion!

# Chapter Three

It didn't take long for Bubba and Beau to become best friends. For one thing, they both went around on all fours. They were both keen on chewing.

Neither one was house-trained. And they could howl to beat the band.

They also had a mutual affection for . . . MUD.
And a mutual disdain for . . . SOAP.

Sister, those two got along.

# Chapter Four

Bubba had the best blankie ever.

He loved its pinky-pink color. He loved its cottony-soft touch. And best of all, he loved its smelly smell.

It smelled just like Beau.

Beau liked that blankie, too. He loved its snappity-snap sound. He loved its toasty-warm warmth. And best of all, he loved its smelly smell.

It smelled just like Bubba.

Sister, that blankie was just right.

Then one day, while Bubba
and Beau weren't looking,
Mama Pearl washed the blankie.

Its pinky-pink turned pale. Its cottony-soft turned soggy. Its snappity-snap turned flat. Its toasty-warm turned shivery.

Worst of all, it smelled like SOAP!

It was a sad day in Bubbaville.

# Chapter Five

Mama Pearl hung the blankie out to dry.

Since she was in a washing mood,
she scooped up Bubba and gave him
a nice hot bath. She used lots of soap.

Then she collared Beau and gave him a bath.
She used lots of soap on him, too.

When it was over, Bubba sat close to Beau. Beau smelled just like soap.

Beau curled up next to Bubba. Bubba smelled just like soap.

Mama Pearl took the dry blankie off the line and handed it to them. It was pinky-pink, cottony-soft, snappity-snap, and toasty-warm. The blankie was back!

Best of all, it smelled just like Bubba and Beau—best friends!